My Colors, My World

Mis colores, mi mundo

Maya Christina Gonzalez

Children's Book Press
San Francisco, California

Sometimes, in the desert where I live,
the wind blows very, very hard.

A veces, en el desierto donde vivo,
el viento sopla muy, muy fuerte.

Desert sand covers everything.
Everything the same color...

La arena del desierto lo cubre todo.
Todo parece del mismo color...

I open my eyes extra-wide to
find the **colors** in my world.

Abro bien los ojos para encontrar
los **colores** de mi mundo.

Of all the colors I find,
I like hot **Pink** the best.
It's the color of the desert sunset.

De todos estos colores, el color que
más me gusta es el **rosa**. Es el color
de la puesta del sol.

I wear **pink** in the morning.
I wear it in the afternoon.
I wear it all the time.

Llevo puesto el color **rosa** por la mañana.
Lo llevo puesto por la tarde.
Lo llevo puesto toditos los días.

On hot days, I go to the shady side of the house.
I make mud pies with squishy **brown** mud and
orange marigold flowers.

12

Cuando hace calor, voy al lado sombreado de la casa. Hago pasteles con el lodo suave, de color **marrón,** y con caléndulas anaranjadas.

I invite **purple** irises to be my guests for tea.
Yellow pollen peeks at me.

Invito a los lirios color **violeta** a merendar.
El polen amarillo no me deja de mirar.

Back on the sunny side of the house,
the cactus grows green and sharp.

En el lado soleado de la casa,
el cacto crece, **verde** y afilado.

In the backyard, I sway on my swing.
I helped my Papi build it and paint it
the perfect shade of **red**.

En el patio, me mezo en el columpio.
Ayudé a mi Papi a construirlo y a pintarlo
de un tono de **rojo** perfecto.

When my Papi comes home from work,
I see his shiny **black** hair.

Cuando mi Papi vuelve a casa del trabajo,
veo su pelo **negro** y brillante.

I love all of the colors in my world.
Every day I watch the hot **pink** sky
turn into dark **blue** night.

Me encantan todos los colores de mi mundo.
Cada día veo el cielo **rosado** convertirse
en noche **azul**.

Photo by Marilyn Smith

The little girl in this book is me. I also modeled her after a doll I had as a kid—a big, round-headed doll my aunt made for me. I dragged that doll around for years because she so reminded me of me, with her big round face.

I faced a number of challenges as a very young person. I turned to my environment to search out my reflection and a sense of belonging. The amazing desert sunset taught me that there was beauty in the world, and that beauty made a difference. I believe this helped lead me to be an artist, and in particular an artist who also paints for children. No matter where we look, inside or outside, there is beauty to greet us. Keep a look out!

Love,
Maya

Maya Christina Gonzalez grew up watching the sky above the Mojave desert in Southern California. She is an acclaimed fine artist whose work has appeared on the cover of *Chicano/a Art*. She has created artwork for nearly a dozen children's books, though this is the first she has both written and illustrated. Maya lives, paints, and plays in San Francisco, California.

First of all I dedicate this book to my fabulous beast Zai, who helped all over the place! Three years old and already an amazing artist. And to Marilyn Smith, whose support, devotion, and out-and-out love made all the difference in the world, on every page and in my heart. Finally, to the kids who read this book. May you know that I was thinking of you—the brave, the scared, the wild and happy—all of you who have had a gray day or a gray time in your life and have found your own brilliance to light your way. May you thrive in all the beautiful colors of your world. —MCG

Story & illustrations copyright © 2007 by Maya Christina Gonzalez

Publisher & Executive Director: Lorraine García-Nakata
Editor / Art Direction & Design: Dana Goldberg
Production Coordinator: Janine Macbeth
Thanks to Jadelyn Chang, Laura Chastain, Ina Cumpiano, Eida del Risco, Maxine
Goldberg, Theresa Macbeth, Patricia Muniosguren and the staff of Children's Book Press.

Library of Congress Cataloging-in Publication Data
Gonzalez, Maya Christina.
[My colors, my world. Spanish]
Mis colores, mi mundo = My colors, my world / Maya Christina Gonzalez.
  p. cm.
Summary: Maya, who lives in the dusty desert, opens her eyes wide to find the color in her world, from Papí's black hair and Mami's orange and purple flowers to Maya's red swing set and the fiery pink sunset.
  ISBN-13: 978-0-89239-221-6 (hardcover)
[1. Deserts—Fiction. 2. Color—Fiction. 3. Hispanic Americans—Fiction. 4. Spanish language materials—Bilingual.] I. Title. II Title: My colors, my world.
PZ73.G589 2007
[E]—dc22   2007005297

Children's Book Press is a nonprofit publisher of multicultural and bilingual literature for children. As a 501(c)(3) nonprofit organization, our work is made possible in part by the AT&T Foundation, John Crew and Sheila Gadsden, the San Francisco Foundation, the San Francisco Arts Commission, Horizons Foundation, National Endowment for the Arts, Union Bank of California, the CBP Board of Directors, Elizabeth Ports, and the Anonymous Fund of the Greater Houston Community Foundation. For a catalog, write: Children's Book Press, 965 Mission Street, Suite 425, San Francisco, CA, 94103. Visit us on the web at: www.childrensbookpress.org

A bilingual color glossary / Un glosario bilingüe de colores:

Pink = Rosa
Red = Rojo
Orange = Anaranjado
Yellow = Amarillo
Green = Verde
Blue = Azul
Purple = Violeta
Brown = Marrón
Black = Negro

Printed in Malaysia by Tien Wah Press
10 9 8 7 6 5 4 3 2

Contact the publisher for sales information. Quantity discounts available for educational or nonprofit use.